Think Global, Act Local

David Keystone

Australia • Brazil • Japan • Korea • Mexico • Singapore • Spain • United Kingdom • United States

Think Global, Act Local

Text: David Keystone
Editor: Vanessa Pellatt
Design: Kerri Wilson
Series design: James Lowe
Photo researcher: Libby Henry
Production controllers: Lisa Porter and Renee Cusmano
Reprint: Siew Han Ong

Acknowledgements
The author and publisher would like to acknowledge permission to reproduce material from the following sources:
Corbis Australia: pp. 8 (top), 21 (right); Department of the Environment, Water, Heritage and the Arts, © Commonwealth of Australia: p. 13 (right); Getty Images: pp. 3 (groceries), 10 (left), 11, 14, 15, 22; iStockphoto: p. 10 (top right); Lonely Planet/Richard I'Anson: p. 23; Newspix/Chloe Erlich: p. 18 (bottom); Photolibrary: pp. 1, 3 (Earth), 4, 5, 7, 9, 10 (bottom right), 12, 13 (left), 16, 17, 18 (top), 19 (main), 21 (left), front and back covers; Shutterstock/Hugo de Wolf: p. 8 (bottom); Shutterstock/Yobidaba: p. 19 (inset); Richard Morden © Cengage Learning Australia: pp. 6, 7 (top), 20.

Fast Forward Independent Texts
Level 14

For product information and technology assistance,
in Australia call 1300 790 853;
in New Zealand call 0508 635 766

For permission to use material from this text or product,
please email **aust.permissions@cengage.com**

ISBN 978 0 17 017981 2
ISBN 978 0 17 017897 6 (set)

Cengage Learning Australia
Level 7, 80 Dorcas Street
South Melbourne, Victoria Australia 3205

Cengage Learning New Zealand
Unit 4B Rosedale Office Park
331 Rosedale Road, Albany, North Shore NZ 0632

For learning solutions, visit **cengage.com.au**

Printed in China by 1010 Printing International Ltd
2 3 4 5 6 7 13

Think Global, Act Local

David Keystone

Contents

CHAPTER 1

Think Global

If people care for the animals, plants, land, water and **atmosphere**, Earth will stay healthy.

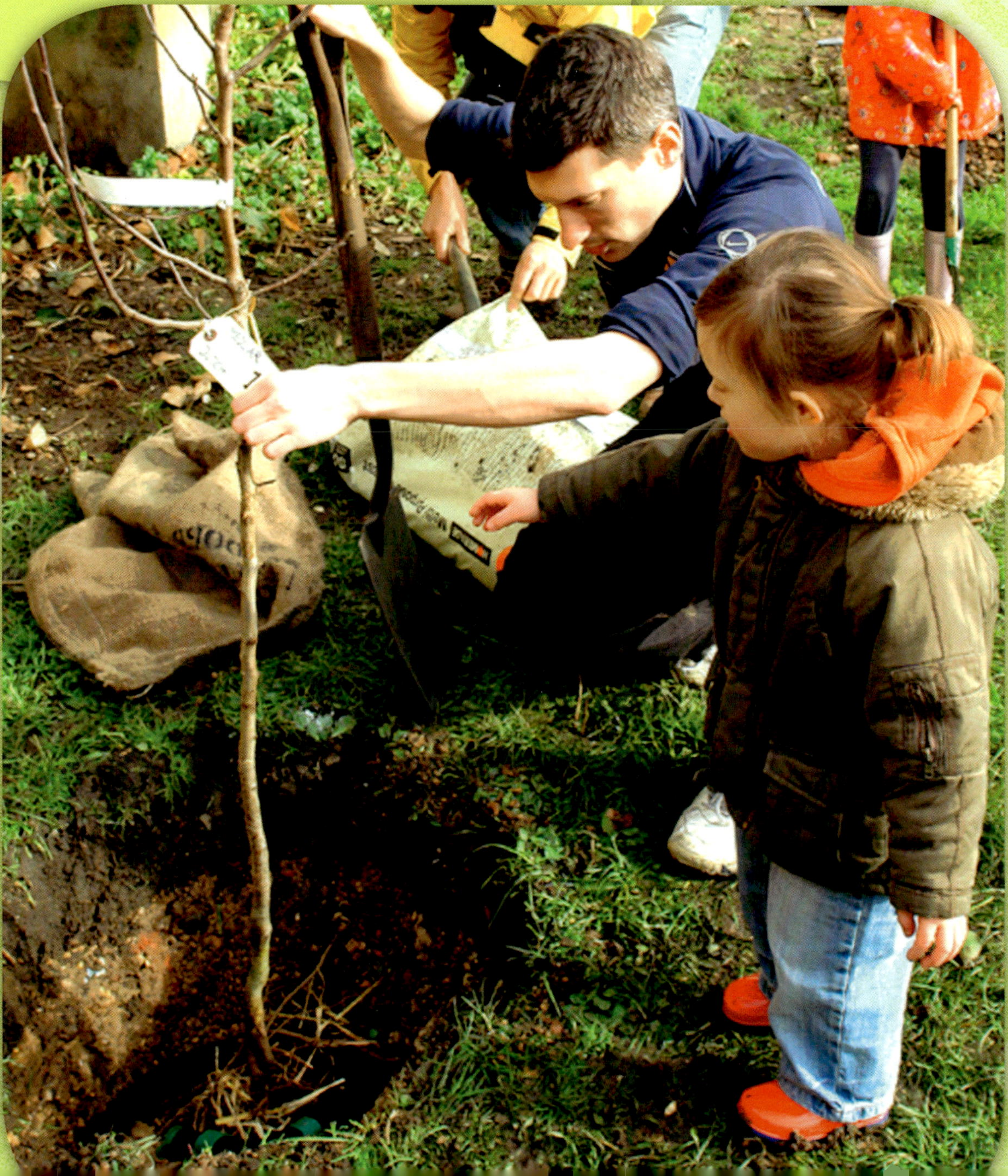

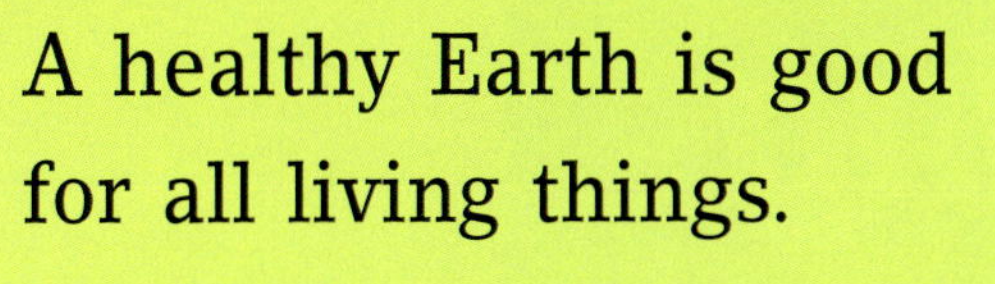

A healthy Earth is good
for all living things.

But right now,
Earth has some **global** problems.

CHAPTER 2

Global Warming

One of Earth's problems is **global warming**.

Heat from the Sun gets trapped in Earth's atmosphere by **greenhouse gases**.

These gases are produced when fossil fuels are burnt.

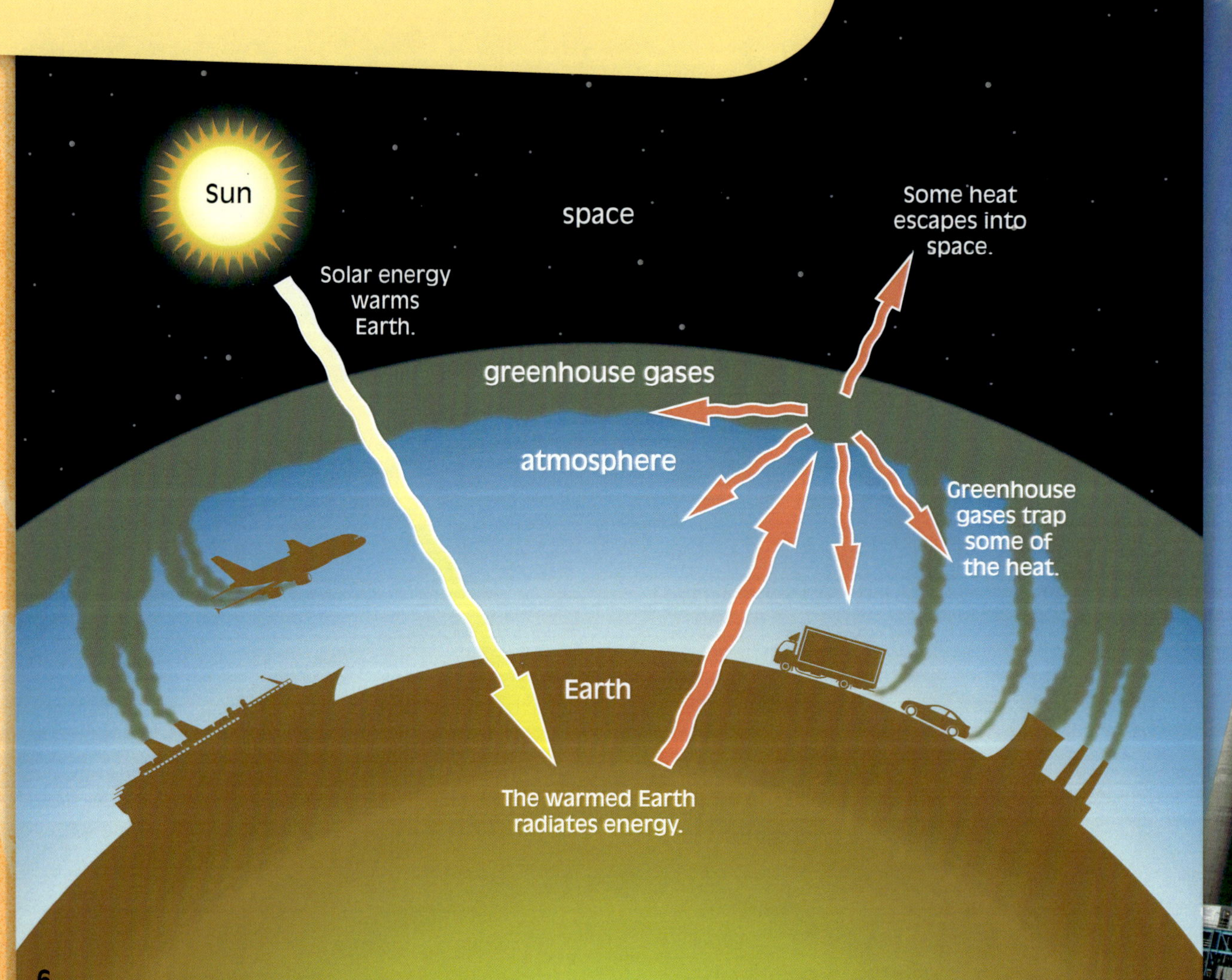

Fossil Fuels

Fossil fuels come from plants and animals that lived millions of years ago.

Factories burn fossil fuels.

Huge forests grew millions of years ago.

The remains of dead plants built up in layers.

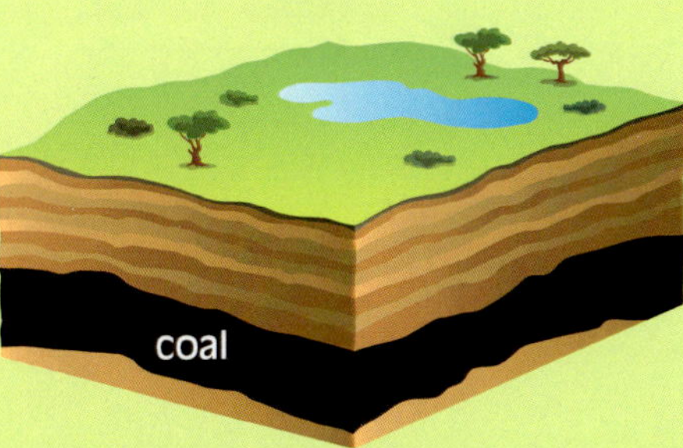

Time and heat turned the layers into coal.

Coal takes millions of years to form.

Over time, these plants and animals have turned into fossil fuels such as coal, oil and gas.

Cars and trucks use petrol, which is made from a fossil fuel.

Burning fossil fuels
produces energy,
which is used to power things
such as factories, cars and lights.

When more fossil fuels are burnt,
more greenhouse gases
are produced.

If there are more greenhouse gases
in the atmosphere,
Earth will get warmer.

Effects on Plants and Animals

If it gets too warm,
it will be hard for plants
and animals to live on Earth.

South Africa's national flower, the King Protea, may become extinct due to warmer temperatures.

The Giant Panda is endangered because it is losing its home. Climate change is one of the reasons this is happening.

If greenhouse gases
are not reduced,
some plants and animals
will become **extinct**.

If Earth keeps getting warmer, this Australian lizard could lose its home by 2050.

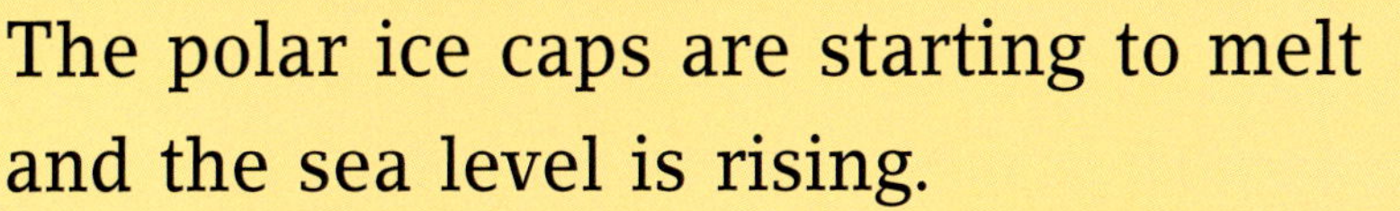

The polar ice caps are starting to melt
and the sea level is rising.

In the future,
more and more land
will be covered by the sea.
People and animals
will lose their homes.

Polar bears could lose their homes if the ice caps continue to melt.

Act Local: Global Warming

Everyone can try to slow down global warming. We can all cut down on how much energy we use at home, school or work.

If less energy is used, it will help to reduce greenhouse gases.

HOW TO REDUCE GREENHOUSE GASES

- Ride a bicycle, walk or use public transport.
- Switch off lights when leaving a room.
- Use low-energy lights.
- Buy appliances that use less energy.

Industries can make a difference to global warming too.

Instead of using fossil fuels, they can work out ways to use alternative sources of energy.

Alternative energy sources, such as wind, water and solar power, do not produce greenhouse gases.

The wind turns these turbines around, making electricity.

It will take a long time to slow down global warming, but people can make a difference.

Landfill

Rubbish is another global problem.

A lot of rubbish is buried in holes in the ground. This rubbish is called landfill.

Making more rubbish means that more land is used for landfill. We are now running out of places to put the rubbish.

Landfill also produces greenhouse gases.

Sometimes rubbish gets into lakes and rivers. If animals or people drink this water, they could get sick.

This water is too polluted to drink.

Act Local: Landfill

Everyone can try
to make less rubbish.

Industries can make less rubbish
by reusing and recycling things.

People can reduce, reuse
and recycle, too.
This means less rubbish
will end up as landfill.

These rubber mats are made from recycled tyres.

Reduce

People can reduce their rubbish. A good way to do this is to buy fewer things.

Buying and selling second-hand things at a market is one way to reuse things.

Reuse

People can reuse things. Or they can give things away, or buy and sell second-hand things.

Recycle

Some rubbish can be recycled. Other rubbish can go in the **compost**. But only rubbish that comes from plants or animals can go in the compost.

This compost bin recycles organic material into compost.

Compost goes back into the ground and helps make other plants grow.

DO

- use cloth shopping bags
- use kitchen items that can be washed
- use both sides of a sheet of paper
- buy things with less packaging
- buy things that are recyclable.

DON'T

- get plastic bags from the supermarket
- use plastic or paper cups
- use only one side of a sheet of paper
- buy things that have lots of packaging
- buy things that are not recyclable.

CHAPTER 6

Making Changes

Everyone can do things
to make Earth a healthy place to live.

By changing some of the things
that we do at home, school or work,
global warming can be slowed down.

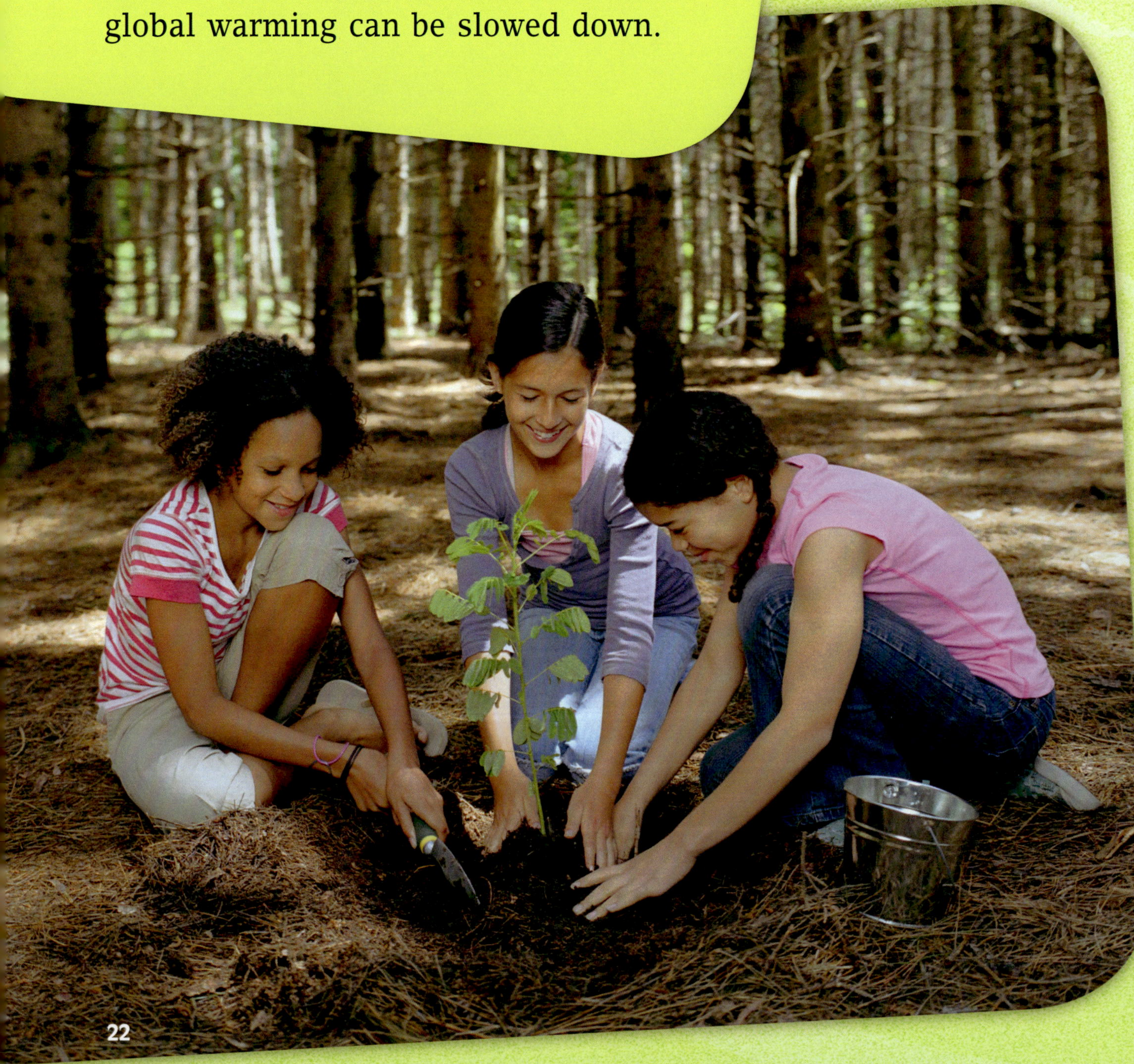

A healthy Earth is good for everyone.

Glossary

atmosphere	the gases surrounding Earth
compost	decaying rubbish used to fertilise gardens
extinct	when a plant or animal is gone from the planet forever
global	worldwide
global warming	the gradual rise in Earth's temperature
greenhouse gases	gases in the atmosphere that trap heat from the Sun

Index